Let's go!

A harvest story

Let's go! A harvest story

Sealaska Heritage Institute
105 S. Seward St. Suite 201
Juneau, Alaska 99801
907.463.4844
www.sealaskaheritage.org

Book design: Nobu Koch

ISBN: 978-1-946019-09-7

10 9 8 7 6 5 4 3 2

This book was made possible through funds from the US Department of Education Alaska Native Education Program Grant PR# S356A140060 *Raven Reading: A Culturally Responsive Kindergarten Readiness Program*. The contents of this book do not necessarily represent the policy of the DOE, and you should not assume endorsement by the Federal Government.

Baby Raven Reads is an award-winning Sealaska Heritage education program promoting a love of learning through culture and community.

Let's go!

A harvest story

By Hannah Lindoff

Illustrated by Michaela Goade

SEALASKA HERITAGE

Go and get a bucket
and come along with me.
Let's hike into the woods
to find a cedar tree.

We'll fill our pail with long bark strips.
If there's time, let's pick spruce tips.

Spring is here, the ground is soft,
watch for puddles as you walk!
Aunty's going to soak the bark,
and weave a hat when nights grow dark.

Go and find a bucket,

we'll take it down the path.

The *yaana.eit** is growing fast,

by the shore we'll find a patch.

We'll fill the bucket with the stalks

and peel a few as we walk.

Yaana.eit is my favorite snack,

with gumboots jarred in seal fat!

* wild celery
yaana.eit – Lingít (Tlingit language)
hlk'íid – X̲aad Kíl (Haida language)
p'iins – Sm'algyax̲ (Tsimshian language)

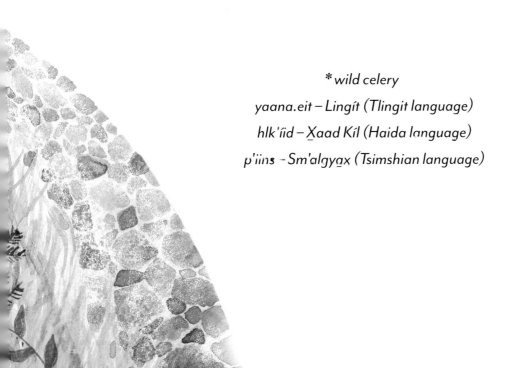

Jump and get the buckets,

the small ones you can carry.

The gentle rains and longer days,

have ripened up the berries.

Let's climb the hill behind our house,

and fill our buckets and our mouths!

Orange, red, yellow, they're all sweet,

for ravens, bears, and kids to eat!

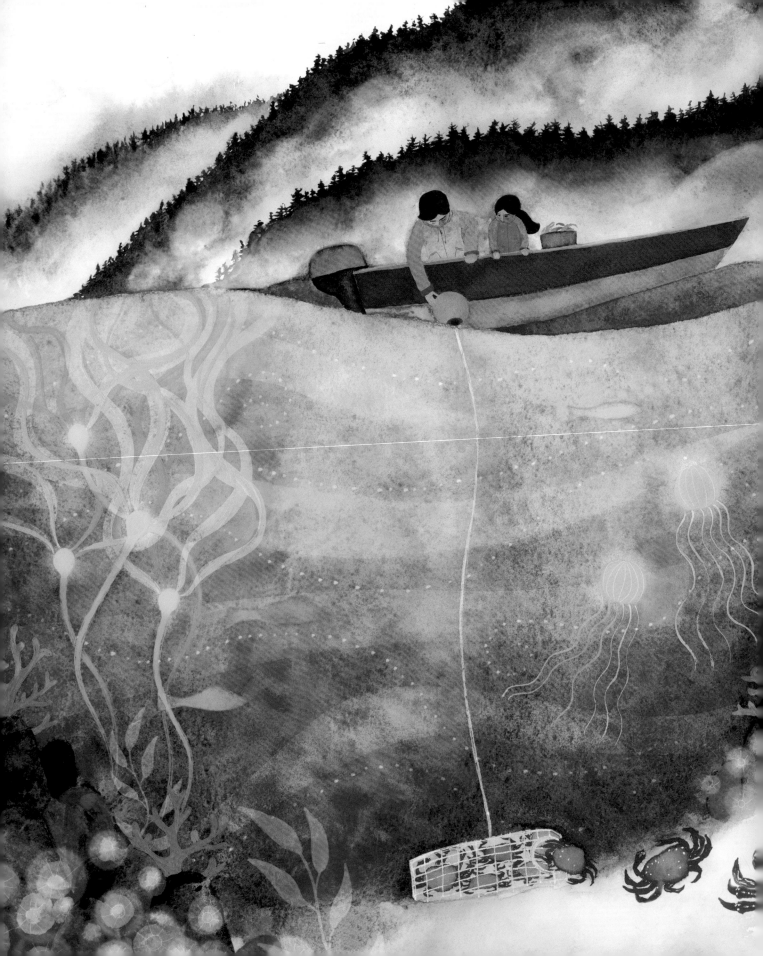

Look inside this bucket,

there's something tasty there!

Look at all these fresh-caught crab,

we've got enough to share!

For sweet white meat in bright orange shells,

our crab pots drift below the swells.

A bright red buoy marks our pot,

it's fun to see what we've caught,

but more fun still is when we eat,

we sit and laugh and pick the meat.

Run and pack a bucket,

pack your long raincoat.

Pack a snack and pack some ice,

we're going on the boat.

When Grandpa's seine makes a set,

just see the salmon fill the net!

Smoke it, bake it, pickle it, dry—

it's always great to eat sockeye!

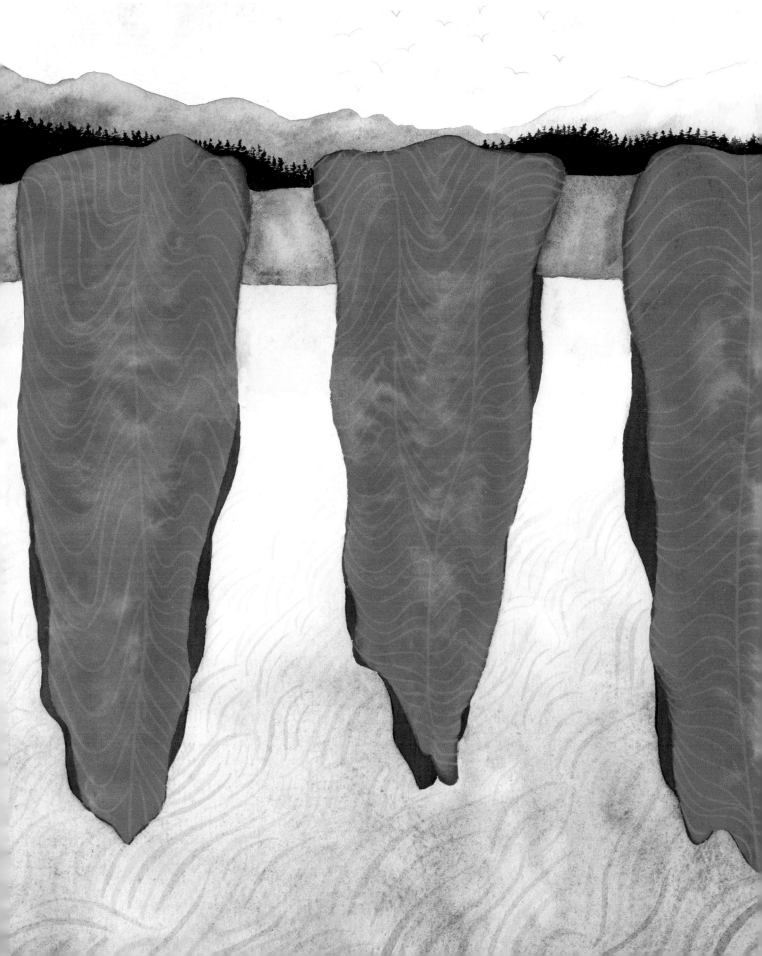

Grab a little bucket,

and come walk with me.

We're going to the meadow,

to pick some wild tea.

The cold has turned some leaves brown,

but look for green plants on the ground.

They smell like summer's musty ripeness,

the long, lush days now behind us.

We'll boil a pot on Grandma's stove,

the best thing for a runny nose!

Go and snag a bucket,

we need one more seat.

Daddy got a great big buck

and now he cooks the meat.

Put a pillow on the pail,

to fit one more around the table.

Call the hunter, say "*Haagú!*" *

to Brother, Aunty, and Uncle too!

*come here
haagú – Lingít (Tlingit language)
hawíit – X̱aad Kíl (Haida language)
yaa 'na gii – Sm'algyax̱ (Tsimshian language)

I'm looking for a bucket.
Can you find one in the dark?
Winter tides draw back the waves
and now the beach lies stark.

Here where ocean has changed to land,
fill a bucket with cockles and clams!
We need a rake, we need warm clothes,
we need a light, now off we go!

Look what's in the bucket!

Herring eggs on branches!

Tiny eggs like yellow beads,

on moccasins we dance in.

Herring spawning in the Sound,

means springtime isn't far from now!

Crunch, crunch, pop, pop.

Let's sit and eat while the Elders talk!

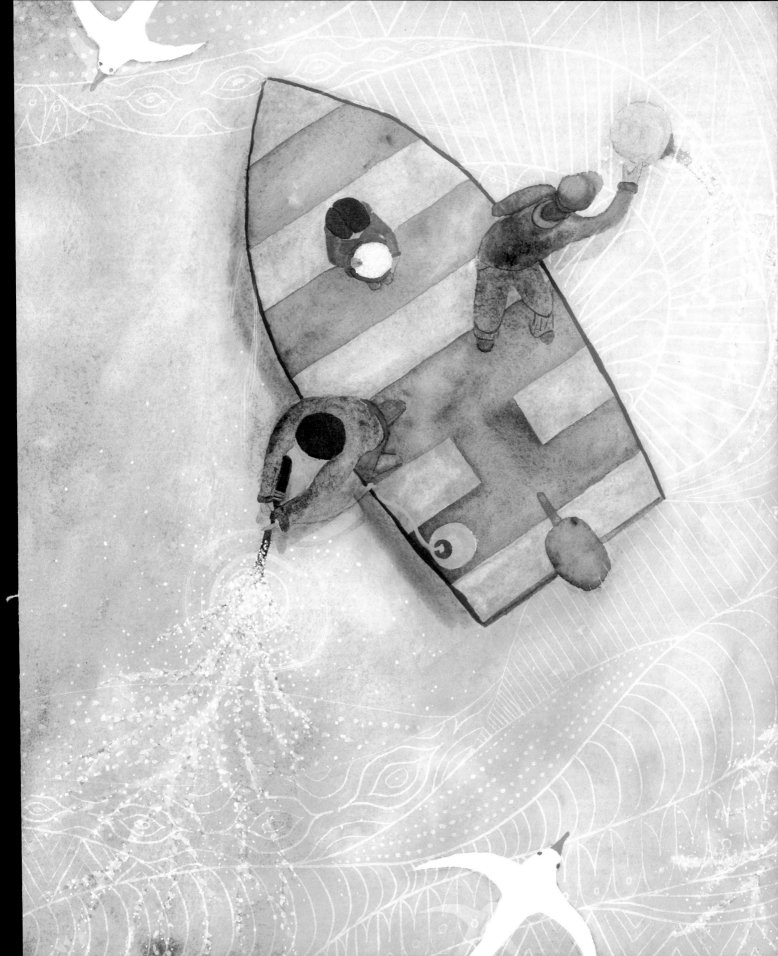

Come and see the cedar hat,

Aunty's just now done!

The land is filled with dewy leaves,

stretching towards the sun.

Oh, go and get a bucket,

and come along with me!

Let's hike into the woods,

to find a cedar tree!

The end

Subsistence in Southeast Alaska

Since time immemorial, the Tlingit, Haida, and Tsimshian people of Southeast Alaska have survived and thrived using what nature provides. We believe all animals, fish, and birds have spirits. We respect the creatures of the tides and beaches that sustain us. We stay in touch with the land, plants, and animals that share this home with us. We strive to live in harmony with the land.

Traditionally, we gathered plants for food, medicine, making rope and nets, baskets and clothing, baby carriers, and diapers. Trees provided shelter, tools, transportation, and firewood for winter warmth. Salmon were caught and preserved for both summer and winter use. Wild berries, rich in vitamins and minerals, are special traditional foods. Currants, soapberries, salmonberries, blueberries, and more are common foods at events and ceremonies. Beach creatures, land animals, and plants nourish us, shelter us, clothe us, and create cultural treasures.

The techniques used to gather food have changed but subsistence hunting and fishing continue to be important today. We continue these traditions, holding deep respect for the gifts that the land provides to sustain and enrich our lives.

We are all linked to one another. Everything has a spirit. We express respect and thanks when gathering what nature provides.

about Sealaska Heritage Institute

Sealaska Heritage Institute is a regional Native nonprofit 501(c)(3) corporation. Our mission is to perpetuate and enhance Tlingit, Haida, and Tsimshian cultures. Our goal is to promote cultural diversity and cross-cultural understanding.

Sealaska Heritage was founded in 1980 by Sealaska after being conceived by clan leaders, traditional scholars, and Elders at the first Sealaska Elders Conference. During that meeting, the Elders likened Native culture to a blanket. They told the new leaders that their hands were growing weary of holding onto the metaphorical blanket, this "container of wisdom." They said they were transferring this responsibility to Sealaska, the regional Native corporation serving Southeast Alaska. In response, Sealaska founded Sealaska Heritage to operate cultural and educational programs.

about Baby Raven Reads

Sealaska Heritage sponsors **Baby Raven Reads**, a program that promotes a love of learning through culture and community. The program is for families with Alaska Native children up to age 5. Among other things, events include family nights at the Walter Soboleff Building clan house, Shuká Hít, where families are invited to join us for storytelling, songs, and other cultural activities. Participants also receive free books through the program.

Baby Raven Reads was made possible through funds from the US Department of Education Alaska Native Education Program Grant PR# S356A140060 *Raven Reading: A Culturally Responsive Kindergarten Readiness Program* running from 2015-2017.

Artist's Statement

As a child I remember the excitement of pulling up the shrimp pots on the boat with my family, the joy of beach fishing with my dad, and the thrill of scrambling through the forests with my mom and sister looking for every last salmonberry, blueberry, huckleberry and, if we were really lucky, every nagoonberry. I can still taste the sweetness of those moments and many more like it. When I first read the poem/story by Hannah Lindoff, I was immediately brought back to those happy memories.

The opportunity to capture the nostalgia of my youth through these illustrations was a rewarding challenge. I am continually inspired by the beauty of the Southeast Alaska environment and being able to use it as a character in this book allowed me to highlight the literal as well as magical and ethereal beauty of the land. I have always loved the ability that art has to create different worlds, and being part of this book has been a dream opportunity to help give life to a special world situated in the place of my upbringing.

Through watercolor, gouache, and digital editing techniques, my goal was to honor these traditional subsistence activities through accurate and detailed illustrations, while also portraying the playful and child-like awe of Southeast Alaska.

-Michaela Goade, 2017

Hannah Lindoff is a life-long Alaskan and adopted member of the T'aḵdeintaan Clan, from the Whale House in Hoonah. In 2017 Hannah will receive her Master of Fine Arts in creative writing from the University of Alaska, Anchorage. She holds a Bachelor of Arts in English from Mary Washington College and is the author of the children's book *Mary's Wild Winter Feast*. She serves on the Juneau Public Library's Publisher Preview Committee for children's literature and is inspired by her family: her husband Anthony and their two children, Marigold and Otto.

Michaela Goade is an illustrator and graphic designer currently residing in Juneau, Alaska. Her Tlingit name is Sheit.een and she is from the Raven moiety and Kiks.ádi Clan from Sitka, Alaska. Raised in Juneau, she spent her childhood in the forests and on the beaches of Southeast Alaska and her artistic style is rooted in the depth and beauty of its landscapes. At the heart of her work, whether it's a logo or book illustration project, is a passion for evocative storytelling. After earning her degrees in graphic design and marketing from Fort Lewis College, she worked as a designer and art director in Anchorage, before embarking on her full-time freelance career and returning to Southeast Alaska.